SLC
89/21

30119 028 931 41 0

D0263097

THIS BOOK BELONGS TO

the trash

To Tillybug – Breathe, believe and everything will come out cute.

First published in Great Britain 2021 by Farshore
An imprint of HarperCollins*Publishers*
1 London Bridge Street, London SE1 9GF

farshore.co.uk

HarperCollins*Publishers*
1st Floor, Watermarque Building, Ringsend Road
Dublin 4, Ireland

Text copyright © Farshore 2021
Interior illustration copyright © Dynamo 2021
The moral rights of the author and illustrator have been asserted.

Special thanks to Rachel Delahaye
With thanks to Speckled Pen for their help in the development of this series.

ISBN 978 0 7555 0128 1
Printed and bound in the UK using 100% renewable electricity at CPI Group (UK) Ltd

1

A CIP catalogue record for this title is available from the British Library.

All rights reserved. No part of this publication may be reproduced,
stored in a retrieval system, or transmitted, in any form or by any means,
electronic, mechanical, photocopying, recording or otherwise, without
the prior permission of the publisher and copyright owner.

Stay safe online. Any website addresses listed in this book are correct at the time
of going to print. However, Farshore is not responsible for content hosted by
third parties. Please be aware that online content can be subject to change
and websites can contain content that is unsuitable for children.
We advise that all children are supervised when using the internet.

MIX
Paper from
responsible sources
FSC™ C007454

This book is produced from independently certified FSC™ paper
to ensure responsible forest management.

For more information visit: www.harpercollins.co.uk/green

SUPER CUTE

FUN IN THE SUN

MAMMA MIRA'S FAMILY RECIPE BOOK

PIP BIRD

Farshore

CHAPTER ONE

Mud Magic

It was dawn and the sun was peeping over the horizon, covering the World of Cute with a sweet honey-glaze. It woke the chime birds, which tinkled like miniature bells across the sky. The crepe flowers slowly unfurled, crinkling and giggling as the rays warmed their papery petals. It was a perfect summer's day.

Micky the mini-pig opened the door of the Piggy-Wiggle Sty and sniffed the air.

He smelled the sweet fragrant puffs from the candy-cotton fields, and the fresh mown grass left by the night-time grass-snippers. But there was something else in the air, too. Something that made Micky grin from ear to ear.

The scent of baking.

Doughy deliciousness wafted on the breeze, along with the growing sound of chitter-chatter and excitement from all corners of town. It was a very special day in the World of Cute.

Micky was just uncurling his tail, which had knotted itself in his sleep, when a herd of fruit squashies flurried past the Piggy-Wiggle Sty. The miniature strawberries, apples and kiwis were very bouncy!

'Hi, squashies!' Micky called, waving. 'You're very lively this morning.!'

'It's the Friendship Festival,' squeaked a kiwi. 'And we're feeling fruity!'

Micky laughed. 'You certainly are. I suppose I'd better get ready!'

The little pig inhaled the delightful air once again before shaking himself to attention. There was lots to do and if he didn't get a piggy-wiggle on, he'd never be ready in time.

The Friendship Festival was a party to celebrate the longest day of the year – the most summery day of summer. In a few short hours, the Straw Breeze Field would be a carnival of music, crafting, picnicking and playing.

cutes. He looked at his pocket watch. They would be arriving any minute!

He suddenly felt a pitter-patter on his head.

'Oh no! Not rain!' he exclaimed, reaching up to feel the droplets. But his head was completely dry. What was going on?

Micky heard a soft giggle. He looked up to see Cami the cloud, blushing with joy, above his head. She was raining hundreds-and-thousands, and a few were stuck to her cloud fluff. She looked like floating candyfloss.

'Did I trick you?' Cami said, still giggling.

'You certainly did, Cami,' Micky said with a grin. 'I thought it was going to rain on Friendship Festival day. That would have been a disaster!'

The most exciting part of all was the Friendship Treat event. Everyone going to the festival took a treat for the Treat Tent, and a Special Guest – chosen on the day – got to taste every single treat before the crowds could help themselves. The treats could be anything, from fruit salads to ice-cream sundaes to banana splits. WHERE FRIENDSHIP SHOWS, ANYTHING GOES! was the festival motto, and everyone was encouraged to make their treats in the company of friends.

Micky, whose day job was guarding the museum, was very keen on rules. Although he was eager to get started on making his special treat, he had to wait for his friends, the super

CONTENTS

'Did you know it hasn't rained on the day of the Friendship Festival for over seventy years?' said a voice. 'Even then, it only rained for 9.3 seconds just before lunchtime and –'

'Sammy!' Micky exclaimed. 'That has to be you. No one else has so many facts on the tip of their tongue. But where are you?'

'Oops! Wait a minute.' There was a flapping sound as Sammy the sloth shook the green camouflage from his fur.

Micky laughed and then turned around as a wobbly cheer rang through the air. A pineapple came racing down the road, faster and faster, squealing with delight, with a scarf streaming out behind her.

'It's Pip! On rollerskates!' Cami said from her lookout position above. 'Stand back, everyone!'

Micky stepped aside as Pip rolled past at full speed, windmilling her arms. She was going so fast, it looked as if she might race right through Micky's garden and out the other side. But there was a thud, then an OW! and – rather suddenly – Pip the pineapple stopped.

She kicked off her rollerskates and got up. 'Oh, Sammy! I'm so sorry!'

Pip had crashed into Sammy and prickled him with her spiky top. He started scratching

his bottom. He had an itch there anyway, so it was quite handy.

'Hey Sammy, I'll scratch it for you!' said someone. 'I'm good at scratching.'

They all looked up to see Lucky the lunacorn on the other side of the hedge, with Dee the dumpling kitty sitting on her back. Dee grinned and flexed her paws to show her sharp claws. 'See?' she said.

Sammy chuckled. 'Thanks for your offer, Dee, but I've got my itchy bottom in hand.'

'It looks like it!' Lucky laughed, jumping over the hedge and landing alongside her friends. 'Are we all here, ready to make and bake our treats for the Friendship Festival?'

The super cute friends all held up their baking bags, bulging with ingredients for their Friendship Treats. '**READY!**' they cheered.

'Almost ready,' Micky corrected. 'We're just waiting for Louis, and . . .' He gave a sharp whistle. A row of piglets marched out of the house. 'Everyone?' said Micky. 'I'd like to introduce my brothers and sisters – Molly, Miles, Marnie, Mei, Millie and Madhu.'

'Hello Molly, Miles, Marnie, Mei, Millie and Madhu!' chorused the super cutes.

Everyone put on their aprons. Micky's siblings did too.

'What shall we bake? What shall we bake?'

said the tiny pigs, squeaking and squealing and cheering.

Lucky tossed her mane. 'I'm doing cupcakes, and I'm hoping that my horn will cover them with glitter. I've got a feeling it will.'

'Of course it will,' Sammy said. 'It's friendship that makes your horn do amazing stuff, and today is all about friendship!'

'I'm going to do some lightning biscuits. Kapow!' Cami shot out a biscuit in the shape of a lightning bolt. It was snatched out of mid-air by a furry muzzle.

'Louis!' the super cutes cheered.

Louis the labradoodle munched the biscuit and gulped it down. 'My icing pen is at the ready to help with decorations!' he said. The artistic dog twitched his magical nose, which could change into pens, pencils, paintbrushes and crayons of any kind and colour.

'You are so clever!' Pip clapped her hands. 'I'm doing an ice-cream pie.'

'Delicious, Pip,' Sammy said. 'Did you know that the first ice cream was invented by Petra the Popsicle in –'

'How about you tell us all about it at the

picnic, Sammy?' Micky said gently. 'We need to get started or we'll never be ready in time. What are you making?'

'Pancakes. Pancakes originated . . . never mind,' Sammy said, quickly pressing his lips together to stop himself from talking any more.

'I'm making a volcano cake,' Dee said, licking her whiskers.

'With real lava?' Micky's brothers and sisters gasped, eyes wide.

Dee winked. 'Wait and see! What about you, wonderful piggies?'

Molly, Miles, Marnie, Mei, Millie and Madhu looked at Micky expectantly. Even though he was the youngest, Micky was clearly in charge.

'The mini-pig family will be making Mud Pie, of course!' said Micky. 'It's a pig's favourite treat!'

'Mud?' Pip said, her pineapple eyes popping. 'You piggies can keep that to yourselves!'

Micky laughed. 'Not real mud. Chocolate! A chocolate-cake bowl filled with a sea of delights. Some bites squidge, others squodge, some goo and others chew.'

'That sounds like a sea I'd like to swim in!' Pip said. 'With my mouth open!'

Micky's eyes twinkled with happiness. This was turning out to be such fun. 'Come on, everyone. Let's go to the Mudporium – my special outdoor kitchen,' he said. 'It's time to create!'

CHAPTER TWO

The Super Special Recipe

The super cutes followed Micky round to the back garden, where there were tables and bowls and rolling pins and even an outdoor oven.

'This is going to be the best Friendship Festival ever!' Cami shivered with happiness and sprinkled a few more hundreds-and-thousands.

'So much space!' Pip said, leaping around the tables. 'It won't be too hot in the kitchen after all, and we can dance while we bake!'

'You've thought of everything!' Lucky said, marvelling at the scene.

'Indeed!' Micky said, his cheeks turning pink. 'Or have I? I'm sure there's something missing...'

But Micky's concern was quickly washed away by a wave of cheering and singing, as his siblings and friends began mixing their treats for the celebration picnic!

Friendship Festival, what a day!
The super cute friends know how to play!
One, two, three, hip hip hooray!

Everyone had been mixing, baking, icing and caking with lots of enthusiasm, as well as having a few food fights. Their aprons were covered in chocolatey smudges, and splats of delicious batter covered the super cutes' skin, fur and faces.

Louis had been practising his swirls and squiggles with his icing-pen nose, and in the flurry of activity he'd managed to draw a moustache and glasses over his own face.

'MROAAAW!' Dee's caramel lava mixture was particularly sticky, and it had glued her

whiskers together. She tipped her head back and let Cami wash it off with special kwik-clean kiwi soap.

'Give me a happy cheer!' Lucky said. 'The sound of your joy will make my horn burst with glittery treats for my cupcakes!'

'YAY!' shouted the others.

Lucky's horn did nothing. There was one voice missing. Lucky's magic wouldn't happen unless ALL her friends were happy.

'What's the matter, Micky?' Lucky asked.

Micky the mini-pig's brothers and sisters had made hundreds of little marzipan pig decorations to put on top of the famous Mud Pie and were squealing with excitement. But Micky was standing at the table, his tail uncurling until it drooped.

'I knew I'd forgotten something . . .' the little pig groaned. 'But I didn't think it would be the actual recipe.'

'What do you mean? You've been baking for ages!' Pip said.

'I know,' said Micky sadly. 'I've tried four times now, and each time there's been too much goo and not enough chew. That means there's a missing ingredient. And I can't work out what it is!'

'Why don't you say the ingredients out loud and see if that helps?' Sammy suggested. 'Piggies? Line up!'

Molly, Miles, Marnie, Mei, Millie and Madhu stood in a row. Micky tapped each one on the head, one by one, as he went through the Mud Pie ingredients.

'Chocolate.'

'Got that!' Molly said.

'Moon-noodle flour.'

'Yep,' said Miles.

'Sublime baking powder.'

'Yes!' said Marnie.

'Cocoa-loco powder.'

'Plenty,' grinned Mei, whose piggy nose was coated in light brown dust.

'Two pink freckled eggs.'

Millie nodded.

'Oil?'

'The finest sunglow oil,' Madhu informed Micky.

Micky tapped himself on the head. 'So what did we miss?' he said. 'We'll have to look in **Mama Mira's Family Recipe Book**. Madhu, could you fetch it from the pantry shelf?'

'Who's Mama Mira?' Lucky asked as Madhu ran into the Piggy-Wiggle Sty to fetch the recipe book.

'Mama Mira was our great-great-great-great grandmother and a brilliant cook,' Micky explained. 'She wrote all her recipes in a book that's been handed down through the generations. Her Mud Pie is legendary. You'll see. I can't wait to show you the book, Louis. It's full of illustrations that she drew herself.'

Madhu ran out with the book. All the cutes gathered round, oohing and ahhing over the hand-written recipes and pictures. Micky flicked through the recipe book until he found Mama Mira's Very Special Mud Pie recipe. Chocolate, flour, eggs, baking powder, cocoa powder, oil . . .

'Of course!' Micky cried. 'I forgot to add the magical mini-marshmallows!'

He ran into the sty. Moments later he ran out

MAMA
MIRA'S
FAMILY
RECIPE
BOOK

again, looking worried and carrying an empty glass jar.

'The magical mini-marshmallows have gone!' he said.

'It wasn't me!' Mei cried.

'Or me,' cried all the other piggies.

'Maybe it was me,' Micky said, scratching his head. 'I do like to munch on a magical mini -marshmallow. Oh dear.'

'We'll just get some more!' said Pip. She did a triple back-flip. 'I can nip to the marshmallow shop in a jiffy!'

'But these aren't just any marshmallows,' Micky said. 'They're special. They have to be picked from the Magic Marshmallow Meadows.

Let's see . . .'

Micky flicked to the back of the recipe book, where Mama Mira had drawn a map of all the places she'd gathered her fine ingredients. The cutes looked over his shoulder.

'Oh,' said Sammy, scratching his top and bottom simultaneously. 'The Magic Marshmallow Meadows are quite a walk.'

'I'll give you a lift, Sammy,' Lucky said. 'With all of us, we'll pick the magical mini -marshmallows in no time.'

'And we'll have fun!' said Dee. 'Every day is an adventure with us!'

'HOORAY!'

CHAPTER THREE

Smells Like Trouble

Taking off their aprons and leaving Micky's brothers and sisters to watch over the cakes, and keep them safe from hordes of fruit squashies and sweet-thief butterflies, the group of friends headed to the Magic Marshmallow Meadows. Micky carried the glass jar to put the marshmallows in.

Sitting on Lucky, Sammy led the way. He was very good at maps. He was also very good at naps, so Pip had to sit beside him and keep him awake with her prickles.

Sammy looked at the path they were on. 'Right,' he said. 'We can either continue on the path or we can cut through the forest, which will be much faster. Seeing as time is ticking and the Friendship Festival will be starting soon, I do think taking the forest route would be best.'

'Good idea, Sammy,' Micky said. 'Come on. If we're lucky, we'll hear some string-a-lings!'

The super cutes changed direction and entered the forest. Liquorice trees towered overhead with rainbow fungi growing up their long trunks, glittering in hues of pink and blue. Soft ferns on the forest floor tickled them softly as they walked.

'It's so beautiful,' said Cami, ducking beneath a branch. 'Ooh! What's that sound?'

A strumming and a humming drifted through the trees.

'It's the string-a-lings!' Dee said. 'Stand still.'

They stopped and held their breath. Tiny guitars with lacy wings fluttered past, playing tunes so sweet it made the cutes' ears tingle. But the string-a-lings' pretty song was interrupted by an ugly screech, and the little creatures vanished in fright.

'What was that?' Dee said.

'Let's find out,' said Louis, bouncing on the spot. He cocked his head as a second screech echoed through the trees. 'It came from that way.'

They trekked on through the forest, until they came across a wooden shack. It had turrets on top, and a red carpet led up the steps to the door. It was like a log cabin pretending to be a castle.

From inside there was high-pitched barking and growling.

The super cutes looked at each other and nodded.

'Clive!' they all said at once.

Trouble was never far behind Clive the chihuahua and his friends, the Glamour Gang. After Clive's dreadful behaviour at the Cuteness Competition and at Sammy's sleepover party, the cutes knew that better than anyone. The last thing they wanted on the day of the Friendship Festival was Clive's unfriendly face and horrid tantrums.

'He sounds upset,' Cami said.

'He always sounds upset!' Dee added.

'No matter how awful that spoilt little chihuahua is, we have to be true to ourselves,'

Lucky reminded everyone. 'And we cutes show kindness, no matter what. We should check he's okay.'

They carefully approached the cabin and knocked on the door. Nobody answered. Clive the chihuahua obviously couldn't hear them over the terrible racket he was making! The cutes stepped into the kitchen. There was flour on the ceiling and broken eggs on the floor, and a very odd smell.

Suddenly, Clive appeared from a pantry, arms full of sugar bags. His hair stuck up like straw and his cheeks were flushed purple with effort. He looked more like a loo-brush than a glamour-pup. He saw them and shrieked.

Clive quickly tried to pat down his hair and smooth his ruffled eyebrows. 'What are YOU doing here?' he said crossly.

'We were just passing and wanted to know if you were okay,' said Sammy. 'We heard the most awful noises.'

'I was singing,' Clive huffed. 'I have a unique style, they say.'

'And we smelled awful smells,' Pip added.

'But we can see you're baking,' Lucky said quickly. She didn't want to hurt Clive's feelings. 'Can we see what you're making?'

Clive's face scrunched up until it resembled a burnt currant bun. 'No,' he yapped. 'It's a secret. I'm going to bake the best cake in the whole World of Cute. You'll see!'

'It's not a competition, Clive,' said Lucky. 'The joy of making Friendship Treats comes from sharing them with friends. Are your friends here?'

'I told the Glamour Gang to go away,'

Clive screeched. 'I don't need any help!'

The worried cutes looked at each other. Clive was very selfish and treated everything in life like a competition. He was so desperate to be the best that he cheated and bullied and even told lies if he thought it would help.

'Clive, do you know what you're doing?' Cami said, trying to dodge the puffs of stink rising from the chihuahua's mixing bowl.

'It's supposed to smell like that,' Clive barked. But his shoulders suddenly dropped and his sharp little voice wavered. 'It's – it's not my fault. I have to make it up as I go along. I don't have a family recipe to follow. My family never HAD any family recipes. People always cooked for US!'

'Perhaps you can be the first one in your family to invent a recipe,' Pip said, trying to jolly Clive along. 'Starting with your, er, lovely cake.'

'I've already thought of that,' Clive snapped, returning to his defiant pose. 'This will be the best cake ever, and people will beg me for the recipe. You'll see. I'm going to make my great-great-great-great-great grandfather proud. This is his castle, you know. He built it to keep all his trophies in.'

For the first time, the super cutes looked around. Beneath the thin layer of flour dust that coated the room, they saw stacks of golden cups.

'What did he win the trophies for?' Sammy

asked, but Clive's head was in the fridge.

'Do I add cheese? I don't know,' said Clive to himself. 'Oh, my great-great-great-great-great grandfather will be so disappointed in me if I don't bake the best cake.'

'IT'S NOT A COMPETITION!'

the super cutes chorused impatiently, but Clive wasn't listening.

'I can't lose. I CAN'T!' Clive yelled the last word. The friends jumped back in alarm.

'Is that your great-great-great-great-great grandfather over there?' Lucky said, pointing at a portrait on the wall.

The portrait showed the haughtiest, snootiest-looking dog they'd ever seen. His little nose pointed at the ceiling, while his beady eyes seemed to follow them around the room. Beneath the picture was a metal plaque with the words:

Keep your eyes on the prize

The cutes looked at each other. That was NOT what Clive needed to see right now. Lucky quickly dabbed jam over the words on the plaque. They moved along the wall to the next painting, which seemed a bit friendlier. This dog had warm, gentle eyes and there was the curve of a sweet smile on her muzzle. In the picture, she was embroidering a decorative dog bone.

'Nice stitching,' Dee said. 'Although I'd have gone with ivory thread. The brown is a bit . . . muddy.'

'Look at the words!' Cami said, floating closer. '"Spread the surprise sunshine of smiles." That's a lovely motto.'

'That's Aunt Augusta!' Clive spat. 'Too soft. Couldn't bark for toffee. No one ever listened to her.'

'Maybe you should,' Pip said. 'The Friendship Festival is all about spreading smiles, after all.'

'Well,' Clive grumbled. 'Making the best cake will make ME smile, so that's all that matters.'

Into his strange-looking mixture, Clive stirred some dog biscuits and pumpkin bites and bones that looked as if they'd been dug out of the garden. The cutes wrinkled their noses, but Clive stood back and looked at his batter with pride.

'It's going to be the best cake at the festival,' he barked.

Lucky realised that Clive wasn't going to listen. He was heading for a big disappointment, just like at the Cuteness Competition. She hated seeing people upset. Even Clive, who made other people feel bad all the time.

'I tell you what would make it even better,' she said kindly. 'Magical mini-marshmallows! We're off the Meadows now, if you want to come with us to collect some?'

Lucky's friends looked at her with disbelief. Why had she just invited the mean little pup to join them on their fun day out?

'Kindness,' Lucky whispered. 'Remember?'

'Clive will probably say no anyway,' Cami whispered back. 'He won't want to hang out with us.'

'All right,' Clive yapped. He whipped off his smeared apron and ran around in a circle. 'I WILL come with you. But *I* get to choose the best marshmallows.'

CHAPTER FOUR

When Micky Gets Sticky

The super cutes waited outside the strange little log-cabin castle while Clive got ready. He was taking ages!

'I wish he'd hurry up,' Micky said nervously. 'There's still so much to do!'

Sammy sighed and looked at his pocket

watch. 'We'll run out of baking time soon.'

'Give him a chance,' Lucky said. 'He's probably nervous. He hasn't spent much time with us as friends before. He might be a little shy.'

To the cutes' amazement, hairdressers and costume designers began to arrive at the little log castle. They marched up the red carpet and through the front door.

The cutes waited some more.

It felt like they had been waiting for HOURS and they were about to give up when, FINALLY, Clive appeared.

There was not a smudge of baking left on him. He'd been washed, scrubbed, dried and dressed. He was wearing a brand-new sequin

46

top and his favourite skirt – a tutu made with fifteen layers of sparkle-net. He pranced into the centre of the red carpet and struck a pose, with one paw in the air and the other on his hip.

'What's he doing?' whispered Cami.

'I think he wants us to clap,' Lucky whispered back.

The cutes clapped politely. The funny little dog bowed and curtseyed and fluttered his eyelashes.

'Something tells me that I'm going to be picked as the Special Guest today,' he yapped, giving a twirl. 'Got to dress for the occasion!'

'Can we go now?' Louis growled.

Clive insisted on riding Lucky to keep his costume clean. Sammy sat alongside and tried to teach him all about the non-competitive origins of the Friendship Festival. Micky held the map at the back of **Mama Mira's Family Recipe Book**, navigating the paths through the Fern Tickle Forest and out the other side.

'Left here!' he called merrily. Then he stopped and scratched his head.

'What's the matter, Micky?' Louis said.

'I'm not sure what's going on,' Micky said. 'The sea is supposed to be on our left, not our right. And look, the hug whales are floating upside down! How peculiar!'

Louis laughed so hard, his four paws left the ground. 'You're holding the map upside down, silly! If you stop looking at the map for a minute you'll see exactly where we are!'

Micky looked up to see that they were standing by the Sherbet Sea. There were the hug whales, turning somersaults in the air and bouncing beach balls on their noses.

'AAAH!' the super cutes sighed.

Even Clive seemed to mellow a little at the sight of the wonderful whales.

'That's better!' Micky said. 'The sea is now on the left, and the Magic Marshmallow Meadows are this way! Hooray!'

Cheering and skipping, the group licked their lips as the sweet sticky smell of those incredible fields got closer and closer.

'It smells amazing,' Cami said, floating higher than she usually did to catch some of the perfume in her cloud fluff. 'Here Clive,' she said, trying to include the grumpy chihuahua. 'Give me a squeeze!'

Clive squished Cami's fluff. The marshmallow

smell washed over everyone. The chihuahua blinked and yapped with surprise.

'I can't wait another moment,' Micky said in excitement. 'Time for a piggy roll. Give me a push, someone!'

Micky lay on the ground and Pip and Sammy launched him down the road. He rolled up the hill,

and down the next hill, and over a rickety bridge before landing with a soft ploof in the Magic Marshmallow Meadows. But he didn't exactly come to a stop. Instead, the bouncy marshmallows sprang him gently into the air. When the others arrived, they couldn't help laughing at the sight of the mini-pig rolling and rising on the pink and

white sweets, snorting happily.

'It's marvellous!' Lucky said, galloping into the magical crop with Clive holding on tight.

'Dee-licious!' said Dee, diving right in.

Louis barked with joy. Pip used the springy marshmallows to perform the highest triple flips she'd ever done, with the softest landing. When she stood up, she had six magical mini-marshmallows stuck on her spiky top.

'Thanks!' Micky said, plucking them off and stuffing them in the jar.

'Over here!' Cami called, floating to the middle of the Meadows. 'This is where the real beauties grow!'

The super cutes gasped. The marshmallows

in the middle had grown glittery decorations – ribbons and bows and stars – and sweet extras, like caramel glazes and toffee chips. Little birds darted in and out of the flowers, and the birds that didn't have their beaks full of marshmallow fluff warbled sweetly.

'Sugar larks!' Dee said. 'I saw an exhibition about sugar larks at the museum. It was one of the exhibits you put together, Sammy.'

'Oh, you saw that!' Sammy blushed. 'I didn't think anyone was interested. They're actually made of dough –'

'I know, Sammy,' interrupted Dee, laughing. 'You explained it in a lot of detail on your information sheet!'

'Sammy does love his facts!' Louis barked.

Everyone laughed – apart from Clive, who was nowhere to be seen.

'What is that chihuahua doing?' Micky asked, putting his hands on his hips.

Cami floated high to get a good view. 'Oh dear, oh dear,' she said. 'Clive's chasing the sugar larks!'

Clive was yapping like crazy. The little doughy birds scattered in terror. As they flapped, flour floated down from their wings. The little chihuahua was quickly covered from his whiskers to his tail.

'Urgh!' he shrieked. 'I've just been groomed by Hairs To The Throne, the finest groomers

in the World of Cute. My fur has been washed, dyed and dried – and now look at it!'

'It wouldn't have happened if you hadn't been chasing the birds,' Lucky said crossly.

But Clive was not going to take responsibility.

'I'm going to get them,' he said, and his angry growl rattled in his throat. 'I'm going to teach them a lesson. No one makes a pedigree look like a chump!'

'Shhh!' Louis said. 'I can hear something . . .'

'That sounds like Micky,' said Lucky. 'Where is he?'

Dee gasped. 'The marshmallows are very high in this part of the field . . . and Micky is very mini!' she said. 'He must have got lost!'

The super cutes pushed carefully through marshmallow plants dripping with the soft mini -treats. There was no sign of Micky anywhere. Even Cami couldn't see anything pig-shaped in the fluffy field below.

'Micky!' she called.

There was a distant oink.

'He's stuck!' Pip cried. 'He needs help. But

if we rush in there we'll get stuck too, and if we all get stuck then we'll miss the Friendship Festival and today will be a disaster!'

'Do some star jumps to release the stress, Pip,' Lucky said. 'Sammy will have an idea. Won't you, Sammy?'

'I already do!' said Sammy. 'Micky?' he called across the Meadows. 'Look up! If you can see Cami, roll towards her. We'll meet you underneath!'

'Got it!' came Micky's faint reply.

The friends could hear the POP and PLUFF of bursting marshmallows as Micky rolled towards them. Glitter pollen filled the air and Dee quickly made a bag and scooped some of it up for later.

'He's coming, he's coming!' said Louis, spotting Micky's little pink feet rolling towards them. 'That's it, Micky!'

'Sammy, your idea worked!' Lucky said, clapping her hands. But Sammy had fallen asleep snuggled into a soft candy cushion.

'I thought he'd been quiet for a while,' Louis smiled. 'Micky, what happened?'

Micky was unharmed, but very, very sticky. He looked like an enormous toffee apple.

'When the flock of birds got startled, they knocked me over and I started to roll and then I couldn't stop and then I got lost and then I started to cry,' he explained, blushing. 'The

tears mixed with the sugar . . . and it turned me into a big ball of glue. It took ages to wade through the marshmallows.'

'You really shouldn't have chased those birds, Clive,' Pip tutted.

'I can do what I want,' Clive said snootily. 'My ancestors probably owned this land and everything in it, including the sugar larks, and –'

'ENOUGH!'

Everyone turned in shock to look at Louis. He was usually so chilled, but the labradoodle's whiskers were bristling and his tail was standing to attention.

'I'm a dog too, so I know how fun it is to

chase,' said Louis fiercely. 'But think of the consequences, Clive! I know if I chase something, it will get scared and ruin the wonderful, peaceful vibe that makes the World of Cute so special. We can all live together happily, if we think of each others' feelings. It's time for you to think about someone other than yourself!'

Clive prickled. He wasn't used to being told off. But something stopped him from having one of his full-blown tantrums. Instead, he swallowed his growl and blinked as if a sweet-thief butterfly had landed on his nose.

'No harm done,' Micky said with a jolly voice 'Now, shall we harvest these delicious marshmallows?'

Clive nodded. The cutes all cheered.

The cheering woke up Sammy. 'Sugar larks flock south in winter where they can feast on tropical banana fritter cakes and mango spangles,' he said. 'What did I miss?'

Lucky laughed. 'Sammy, you are funny! I'll tell you all about it while we collect marshmallows for Micky's Mud Pie.'

CHAPTER FIVE

Yum For All, and All For Yum!

With a basket full of magical mini-marshmallows, the cutes made their way back to Micky's mud kitchen. Despite the disagreement about the sugar larks, Clive insisted on coming back to help. The cutes wondered if it was so he could take a look at the 'competition'. But that didn't matter. The most important thing was getting Micky and his family's Mud Pie baked and ready for the Friendship Festival.

Everyone helped get the choco-mud mixture just right. They added the moon-noodle flour, chocolate, cocoa-loco powder, pink freckled eggs and sunglow oil.

'And now for the special ingredient!' Micky called, holding aloft his jar of sweet magical mini-marshmallows.

'Pour them in!' Pip squealed.

Everyone started chanting. 'POUR THEM IN! POUR THEM IN! POUR THEM IN!'

Micky stopped. 'Where's Mei?' he asked.

'Inside, hiding under the bed,' said Marnie. 'It WAS her that ate all the magical mini-marshmallows.'

Micky trotted inside and returned holding his sister's hand.

'Mei, would you do the honour of adding the final wonderful ingredient to Mama Mira's Mud Pie?' he said.

Mei's lip trembled. 'But I don't deserve it.'

'Yes, you do,' Micky said. 'It's the Friendship Festival. Today, above all days, we should know

that friends and family and forgiveness are the greatest things on Earth.'

'And fabulous outfits!' said Clive. 'I have a fifteen-layer sparkle-net tutu, you know.'

Everyone ignored him.

Mei's worried little face stretched into a wide, happy grin. She let out a little snort. 'Thank you, Micky!' she said, taking the jar.

The jar was heavy and Mei's hand wobbled. Rather than sprinkle them in one by one, they fell in a big lump. Cami quickly whipped up a breeze that separated the marshmallows and made them pitter-pat like yummy rain droplets into the mud mixture.

'HOORAY!'

The cutes stirred the mixture together and popped the Mud Pie in the oven for fifteen minutes. That gave everyone time to add the finishing touches to their own cakes and creations. Icing drops and sugar flowers were scattered over the delicious treats, and Louis made his nose into an ice-cream pen for Pip's ice-cold pie.

'What a wonderful scene!' sighed Lucky. 'All my friends baking and laughing and preparing for one of the greatest days ever on the Cute Calendar! I can feel my horn tingling with magic, ready to conjure up the tasty glitter for my cupcake topping!'

She closed her eyes to soak up all the sounds of fun and ... and ...

'That's disgusting, Pip!' screamed Clive. 'And what do you call that, Sammy? A pancake? It looks like you stepped in something nasty and put it on a plate!'

The little chihuahua was strutting around the mud kitchen, picking faults with everyone's treats. Lucky's friendship tingle disappeared. This was typical of Clive, making others feel bad in order to make himself feel better! As for his own cake, it was solid and grey, like a rock. A bad-smelling rock.

Lucky sighed. The moment had gone. It looked as if there'd be no glitter topping for her cakes after all.

Dee noticed Lucky's face and pulled a bag

from her fur pockets. Inside was glitter pollen from the Magic Marshmallow Meadows. She sprinkled it all over Lucky's cupcakes and gave her a big warm cuddle.

'Thank you, Dee,' Lucky sniffed. 'You make everything better.'

'The Mud Pie is ready!' Micky called.

Everyone gathered around to see the incredible creation. The chocolate sponge bowl was rich and dense, and inside it was a gloopy sea of scrumptiousness beneath a firm crust of sweet frosting. The lumps and bumps of tasty magical mini-marshmallows poked through. It looked like a mud puddle, but it smelled like heaven!

'It's perfect!' Pip squealed.

'I can smell the chocolate from up here!' Cami sang.

'Chocolate and sweets were the first currency in the World of Cute, did you know?' said Sammy. 'Cutes gave each other gummy

bears, fruit-hoops and chocolate coins in payment. Sometimes covered in edible gold -leaf.'

'That's fascinating, Sammy,' Cami said.

'Did they look anything like this?' Dee said, whipping out some gold leaf and wrapping it around some jellied pineapple chunks.

'I'll take those,' Clive said, snatching the golden chunks from Dee's paw and stuffing them in his pockets. 'My ancestors invented ALL the treats in the world, so by rights, it all belongs to me.'

'I don't think that's entirely true,' Sammy said.

'Let him think what he wants,' Louis sighed.

'What's important is that treats exist, and we have friends to share them with. Now, isn't it time we went to the Friendship Festival?'

At that moment, a chiming sound hit their ears with a tinkle and a tingle, like a hundred little bells blowing on the breeze.

'The Friendship Festival! It's beginning!' Pip shouted. 'Come on, everyone, let's go!'

'Single file, single file,' Micky said to his siblings as they all rushed out.

The happy group skipped towards the Festival, their arms filled with boxes of cake and plates of pancakes and dishes of deliciousness.

Whoa! When they reached Straw Breeze Field, the sight took their breath away. The

Friendship Festival was a riot of colour. Bunting fluttered on the breeze. Tent canopies billowed, incredible smells and sounds coming from each one. Music was everywhere. There were cupcake marching bands, jelly jazz bands, oompa-tato bands, and on the centre stage was

Hairbrush 100 – a glamorous pop band led by Hannah the hairbrush, who was a bit of diva but had the voice of an angel bird.

'I've never been here with so many of my best friends before,' Lucky said. 'It's like a dream!'

'What do you think, Micky?' Louis asked.

Micky was so amazed by the sight of the Festival, he couldn't even oink. Pip pointed to his tail, and everyone laughed. The little curl was spinning faster than a Catherine wheel.

Clive tutted. 'I don't know what you're all so amazed about,' he said. 'I have birthday parties way more glamorous than this!'

'Sure you do, Clive,' Pip growled.

Lucky wondered if Clive just pretended he had a wonderful life to make himself feel better.

'Would you like to hang out with us at the picnic, Clive?' she said.

'No,' said Clive with a sniff. 'I've just spotted my REAL friends. See you later!'

The chihuahua trotted off towards the Glamour Gang, who cheered when they saw him.

'I wish the Glamour Gang would treat Clive less like a movie star and more like a normal pup!' said Louis.

But there was no time to worry about Clive now. The festival was buzzing, and the friends couldn't wait to be part of it.

Cutes streamed past in every direction, faces wide with wonder and voices loud with excitement. Toby and the telephone family rang on seeing the super cutes, and Suki and all her little succulent pots stopped to say hello. A huge crowd of popsicles stopped to lick their

lips at Pip's ice-cream pie, and Pip danced with delight in the chilled air around them.

'Where do we put the cakes?' Dee said, trying to stop her lava cake getting knocked by the crowds.

'I can see the Treat Tent,' Cami called. 'Follow me.'

'Single file! Single file!' Micky called.

The cutes giggled at Micky's bossy voice. But he was right. Walking behind each other, they could protect their precious treats and not get lost.

They snaked their way through the cute crowds to the Treat Tent, where everyone was placing their offerings. What a variety!

Strawberry surprise, barley cookies, banana granola and a huge pile of carrot creams, which were vanishing, thanks to the baby funny bunnies under the table scoffing them with glee.

'The Special Guest gets first taste, you naughty bun buns!' Lucky said, moving the carrot creams out of the funny bunnies' reach.

'Everything looks so good,' Sammy said. 'I've got my eye on those tree-sap flapjacks.'

'And I've got my eye on the prize,' Clive said, zooming up to the table on his friend, the scooter. He shoved aside all the plates. 'I'm putting MY cake right in the very centre, where it deserves to be.'

'For the last time, Clive, there IS no prize,'

Lucky said with a sigh.

'That's what YOU think!' yipped Clive.

'Well!' said Louis as Clive and the scooter zoomed away. 'That's the last time we should try and show kindness to that jumped-up little pup!'

CHAPTER SIX

A Chihuahua Too Far-Far

The Treat Tent was getting busy as cutes rushed to display their plates of goodies and have a good look at everyone else's creations.

'You should take a look around the rest of the Festival,' Cami told her friends as she floated above their heads. 'It's all so wonderful!'

Everything at the Friendship Festival was busy and bustling. Thirsty cutes gathered round the pink lemonade stalls, and Cookie the clown was entertaining everyone with his balloon-twisting skills. He created rhinos and elephants and hippopotami, which made bellowing animal noises as they landed in the crowd's laps.

There was a sudden roar of applause on the other side of the festival.

'It's the Diamond Stage,' Cami reported. 'They're introducing this year's Special Guest!'

'I wonder who will it be?' Dee said.

'Let's go and find out!' Louis said with excitement. 'If it's me, shall I play it cool, or wag my tail a hundred miles an hour?'

'Do whatever comes naturally,' Cami said, raining little hairbrushes. 'Ooh! I don't know why I did that!'

'Quick!' Pip shouted. 'Pineapple roll! Someone push me.'

Micky gave her a push, but Pip's prickles caught on the soft grass and she didn't go far.

'Maybe I should leave rolls to pigs,' Pip giggled. 'And hot dogs.'

They got to the stage just as the Drumming Diddlers did their exciting drum-roll to introduce the Special Guest. A voice boomed from the speakers.

'To open this year's Friendship Festival here at Straw Breeze Field, we welcome our

Special Guest . . . Sushi Suzy!'

There was wild applause as the smiley sushi cute joined the drummers on stage. Sushi Suzy was wearing a bright yellow dress made of fresh ginger and shiso leaves. She was famous for dressing according to the mood, and on the longest day of the year with the sun beaming down so beautifully, she couldn't have chosen better.

Sushi Suzy did a twirl, fanning spiced ginger fragrance across the crowd. There was a big cheer, especially from all the other sushi cutes. The ginger beers whooped wildly, and there was an extra big hurrah from Natalie the noodle bowl. It was clear who the big fans of ginger were here!

'That dress is awful,' Clive said loudly.

'Awful!' repeated the Glamour Gang.

'Totally lacking in style!' Clive shouted.

'Lacking in style!' the Glamour Gang echoed.

Sammy got ready to camouflage himself, creep up on them and give them a good poke in the bottom, which he was very good at. All the attention was on the stage, where Suzy was skipping around behind a glittering red ribbon tied from one side of the stage to the other. The crowd clapped along.

'Hello, World of Cute!' Suzy called. 'I am honoured to be Special Guest, and I declare the Friendship Festival well and truly . . . open!'

Suzy beckoned Sirius the scissors on

stage. On the count of three, Sirius snipped the ribbon and everyone cheered.

'Wait up, Suzy!' shouted someone.

It was Guac the Avo-cuddle. He scurried on to the stage and whispered something in Suzy's ear. Suzy's eyes widened.

'Everyone!' she called. 'Because it's so warm and we don't want things melting everywhere, we're going to do the Friendship Treats first! Everyone to the Treat Tent!'

The crowd headed back towards the tent. The super cutes held hands and squealed with happiness as they skipped across the field. They couldn't wait for everyone to taste their plates. They had made everything in such a brilliant atmosphere of friendship that the flavours were bound to be incredible!

As they got closer to the Treat Tent, they were met by a ripple of gasps and an air of despair.

'What's going on, Cami?' Lucky said.

Cami floated into the tent to find out. She came back again, her white cloud-fluff grey and miserable. 'There's been some sort of accident,' she said. 'The Friendship Treats are ruined!'

Clive came riding over in the basket of the scooter, followed by the rest of the Glamour Gang: a pizza slice, a muffin and a snail.

'What a shame,' Clive said smugly. 'All your pretty cakes smashed to pieces with a tennis racket.'

Lucky frowned. 'Clive, do you know something about this?'

'Me?' said Clive. 'No, not at all. Got to go now. Bye!'

The smirking scooter powered away and Clive waved toodle-oo with a glint in his beady eye.

'Have they really destroyed all of the amazing treats?' Pip said in shock.

'Let's go and see,' Micky said. 'Perhaps we can fix it.'

The cutes slowly approached the table where they'd laid their wonderful treats – treats they'd spent all morning chasing ingredients for.

OH NO!

Cami's lightning biscuits were gone. Dee's lava cake had well and truly erupted. Pip's ice-cream pie was a puddle, and Lucky's cupcakes had indeed been smashed to pieces with a tennis racket, which was still sticking up out of the remains.

'Our Mud Pie!' Micky wailed. The plate had been tipped upside down and stamped on,

making the pie look as appetising as a fresh cow pat.

'And look whose cake hasn't been touched,' Louis growled.

In the centre of the table, Clive's rock cake was the only treat standing. And it seemed to have grown some decorations. It was now prettied up with Lucky's glitter pollen and Micky's marzipan models and a little yummy glaze from Dee's caramel lava.

The sound of sobbing echoed loudly around the field. Sushi Suzy still had the microphone in her hands and was giving little hiccups of upset.

'It was my year to be Special Guest,' she

sniffed, gazing at the ruined Treat Tent. 'And I wanted it to be so, so special. I was so looking forward to tasting all the treats . . . but now I can't eat them!'

'There is one magnificent cake left for everyone to enjoy!' said a high-pitched voice in the crowd. It had a strangely yappy tone to it.

'Wait! Wait!' shouted Micky.

Everyone fell quiet and watched as Micky the mini-pig scrambled onto the treats table and stood next to Sushi Suzy.

'Can I just say something?' he whispered.

Suzy gave him the microphone. 'Go ahead, Micky.'

Micky cleared his throat. 'It looks like a very

unfriendly act has happened here,' he said into the microphone. 'Although we can't change it now, we can fix it if we all help each other. After all, that's what the Friendship Festival is about. So, let's get creative and help each other make incredible new treats from the mess that's left. And then everyone can enjoy them!'

Micky stopped talking and blushed as he saw all the faces looking at him.

'No! I'm the winner!' squeaked a very snippy voice. 'Uh, I mean this cake is the BEST one for everyone to enjoy!'

Suzy took the microphone back and patted Micky on the head. 'Micky's suggestion is right at the heart of what the Friendship Festival is all about,' she said. 'So, all you wonderful cutes out there? Grab your friends and build your treats. You have one hour to make NEW friendship delights for one and all!'

Clive let out a shrill growl of frustration, but it couldn't be heard over the hubbub of excitement that had gripped the Friendship Festival. Cutes teamed up and gathered round tables, collecting bits and pieces from the giant treat crash.

The super cutes looked at each other and smiled.

Dee stretched out her paws and flexed her claws. 'Let's make!' she said.

CHAPTER SEVEN

Second Chances

With all the treats broken into so many pieces, there were lots of ways to get creative! There were chocolate crisps, honeycomb shards, meringue crumbles and oat slices. There were marzipan blobs and icing splodges.

'What a mess!' Pip sighed.

'A beautiful mess,' Dee said, delighted. 'It's

like an art workshop just waiting for an artist.'

'If there's any left for us to get arty with,' Pip said anxiously.

The treaty pieces were disappearing fast. Some of Lucky's cupcakes were disappearing to help make someone else's creation.

'Where's Sammy?' Micky said. 'He was here a second ago . . .'

'Sorry!' Sammy's camouflage fur had gone dark brown, just like the pile of chocolate cake behind him. He turned bright orange. 'Is that better? Or shall I go peach? Or apricot, maybe?'

Pip giggled. 'Oranges, peaches and apricots! Yum!'

'Wait! You've given me an idea,' Micky said.

'Why don't we make something fruity and fresh to represent summer?'

'That's a brilliant idea, Micky!' Sammy said.

'Think of the colours,' said Cami dreamily.

'And the vitamins!' Pip said doing a flip and landing on her head. 'Ouch.'

'And the fibre,' Sammy said, scratching his bottom.

'A Fruity Friendship Cake!' Cami puffed up with happiness and sprinkled down juice-filled gummy hearts. Louis tried to snap them up before they popped in the air with happy squeals.

'What a lovely idea,' Lucky said, clapping her hooves. 'A Fruity Friendship Cake.'

'But it needs a surprise,' Dee said. 'Everything is better when there's a surprise!'

'We'll think of something,' Lucky said. 'Let's start by building the base.'

The friends collected chunks and slices of treats and began to create a base for their cake creation. It was wide as a wagon wheel, and in each bite there would be a crunch or a crisp with a spongy bounce and a caramel ooze.

'We need just a little more, I think,' Sammy said. 'Micky, pass me that big chunk of Mud Pie.'

Dee clapped her paws together. 'And finally, it's time for a fruit layer. Gather up all the fruity bits and pieces you can find.'

The super cutes rushed off to look for some fruity fun – apart from Louis, who stayed where he was, looking sad.

'What's up, Louis?' Sammy asked, patting his friend.

'I can draw, but I'm not very good at making things,' said Louis with a sigh. 'I've done nothing to help. I can't even sniff out fruit very well.'

Sammy scratched Louis affectionately behind the ear. 'Did you know that fruit squashies are attracted to fruit?' he hinted.

Louis looked puzzled. 'That's interesting, Sammy,' he said. 'But how will it help?'

'Think about it,' Sammy suggested. Then

he crawled under the bake table for a nap.

'Think about it,' Louis repeated to himself.

He suddenly saw a bunch of giggling fruit squashies bouncing towards the hedgerow at the far end of the field.

'They know where fruit is!' Louis exclaimed, and ran after them.

The cute friends all trooped back to the treats table, looking glum.

'Most of the fruit got completed squished,' Pip moaned.

'How on earth are we going to make a Fruity Friendship Cake without fruit?' Lucky said.

They all heard the sound of frantic barking. With his tail wagging, Louis was winding his way through the crowd. In his mouth was a basket . . . and it was brimming with berries!

'Harvest time!' Louis declared, setting the basket down.

'Oh, well done, Louis!' Sammy said with a smile.

'So we've got all the ingredients!' Lucky said happily. 'But how are we going to make it surprising?'

Cami suddenly floated into view above their

heads. Her fluff was flashing dark blue with anger. Sammy reached up to give her a cuddle, and she rained sharp icy hail.

'Ouch!' the cutes cried.

'Sorry, everyone,' Cami said. 'I can't help it. I'm just so angry! I just spotted Clive and the Glamour Gang. I got as close as I could by disguising myself as a normal cloud and listened to their conversation. They heard our plans for a Fruity Friendship surprise, and are planning to ruin it. That rotten snail has fetched along all his brothers and sisters, and told them that there's an all-you-can-eat fruit competition!'

'Snails have even more brothers and sisters than pigs!' Micky wailed.

'They're going to munch through every piece of fruit we've got!' Dee mewed.

Micky started sobbing. 'I wanted this to be such a special day with my very best friends,' he sniffed. 'But Clive and the Glamour Gang are going to ruin everything!'

'Don't take it personally, Micky,' said Lucky. 'Clive will do anything to be the centre of attention. It's all my fault for trying to include him.'

'They're coming!' Cami whispered. 'The snails! They're coming!'

'When they see this fruit, they'll chomp it all up,' Pip cried.

'Then . . . we'll hide it!' Dee said, her eyes widening.

The little dumpling kitty collected pieces of meringue and smashed them into smithereens with her busy little paws until there was nothing left but a pile of powder.

'Dee, what –' Louis began.

'Shhhh!' Micky interrupted. 'Let Dee work. When it comes to making and crafting, she always knows what she's doing.'

Dee began to roll the berries in the meringue powder until they were all covered in the fine sugary dust. Not a single raspberry red or blueberry blue could be seen beneath their white coats.

'Now, Cami,' Dee said. 'When I throw the berries to you, freeze them and hang on to them, okay?'

'Got it!' Cami said, her cloud flushing a cool ice-blue.

Dee tossed the fruits. Cami froze them in mid-air. Now they hung on fine icicles from her underside, high up and safely out of reach.

Just as Cami froze the last berry, Clive, the Glamour Gang and the fruit-snatching snails turned up.

'Go on, kids,' the mean snail commanded. 'Find the fruit!'

The little snails slid all over the place, trying to catch a taste of a fruity trail, but they returned from their hunt with nothing on their tongues or in their bellies. The first one shook his head and made his eyes wobble.

'No fruit,' he complained.

Sammy crouched down. 'If you're looking for fruit, follow the fruit squashies,' he told the snails. 'I saw them heading out of the gate towards Fern Tickle Woods. If you hurry, you'll catch them up.'

Before Clive or any of his gang could stop them, the little snails trundled towards the exit gate as fast as their little rippling feet would allow. Clive's whiskers quivered. His little legs trembled with fury.

'Nothing to see here, Clive,' Louis barked.

'Why are you being so MEAN!' Clive yapped back.

The chihuahua's bottom lip wobbled.

Perhaps he really had enjoyed spending time with the super cutes, after all. Then the little dog walked away with his tail between his legs.

'Phew!' Dee said. 'Now, we've got to hurry. Sushi Suzy will be back any minute to taste the second-chance treats. We managed to save the fruit, but we still need the surprise!'

Cami floated above the Fruity Friendship Cake and rained down the iced fruit in little peaks. They sparkled brightly around the cake. As the sun began to melt the ice, the fruit colours glowed from underneath like precious jewels.

'Quickly!' Lucky said. 'Suzy's at the table next to us!'

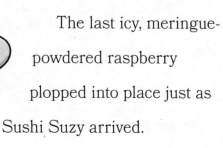

The last icy, meringue-powdered raspberry plopped into place just as Sushi Suzy arrived.

'Hello cutes,' said Suzy. 'What have you made for us?' When her eyes rested on the Fruity Friendship Cake, she gasped. 'It's delightful. Delightful!'

She took a small sliver of Fruity Friendship Cake with its cold fruit top and nibbled it. Her eyes sparkled.

'That is so, so good,' she cried.

The sushi cute continued along

the line, looking at and trying all the new treats on display. She declared all of them delicious – but then she returned to the Fruity Friendship Cake and raised her microphone.

'Friendship Festival, is everyone having fun?' she called.

There was a giant cheer in response.

Suzy smiled. 'Good, because in a minute you're going to have some YUM!' she said. 'And although this is NOT a competition, I have chosen my Treat of the Day. I have picked it for two reasons. One, because it looks like a summer crown, studded with the prettiest juicy jewels grown right here in the World of Cute. And two, because it's made by a group of cutes that really show us what it means to be friends.' Suzy gave a happy twirl in her ginger dress. 'Where friendships show, that's when you know!'

She pointed to the cake with a dark chocolate bottom and a glistening top like a bejewelled crown. 'Everyone put your hands and paws together for Cami, Pip, Sammy, Lucky, Micky, Louis and Dee!' she said.

While the cutes were hugging each other and the festival crowd was cheering, no one saw two little paws reach across the other side of the table until it was too late. Clive wrapped his arms around the cake.

'Hey, get off that cake!' Micky yelled.

'I just want to say something,' Clive said.

'Step away from the cake, Clive,' Cami said in a soft, low voice.

Clive clutched on to the cake tightly and closed his eyes.

'Not again,' Micky wailed with a blubbing sob.

'LET ME SPEAK!' Clive yapped.

Just as Lucky's horn could do incredible

things with the feeling of friendship, it also reacted when anyone hurt her pals. Her horn suddenly released a swarm of angry sherbet popcorns, which flew around Clive's head like wasps around a donut.

'Get them off me!' Clive yelled, thrashing his head from side to side and flinging his little arms up . . .

And into the air flew the Fruity Friendship Cake!

CHAPTER EIGHT

Summer Surprise

'Family!' shouted Micky the mini-pig. 'Piggy roll!'

The shout was so loud that everyone leaped back. It was a good job too. Micky was rolling through the crowd at full speed – and behind him rolled his brothers and sisters!

The row of rolling piggies sped toward the

spot where Clive had been standing (the little chihuahua was now cowering under the table). Just in time, Micky and his siblings jumped up in a perfect circle and raised their arms. The huge plate landed perfectly on their upturned trotters. The cake was safe, and not a single piece of fruit had been lost.

The crowd cheered. The Fruity Friendship Cake was saved!

Clive grabbed at Suzy's ginger dress with his chocolate-covered paws to pull himself out from under the table. There were still tears in his eyes.

'I just want to say something, pleeeeease,' he whined.

'Not now, Clive,' said Suzy. 'Everyone to your picnic blankets to collect your plates!'

As a symbol of togetherness in the World of Cute, everyone had their first taste of the Friendship Treats at the same time. The cutes quickly put cookies and slices of niceness on their plate and returned to their picnic rugs.

Their tummies rumbled as they waited for the blow of the Friendship Horn.

Suzy waltzed on to the stage and spoke into the microphone. 'Every cake and treat has been shared out, ready for this very special moment, and –'

'Wait!' Clive yapped.

Everyone groaned.

What did Clive want now?! Wearing his cake-stained fifteen-layer tutu, Clive climbed on to the stage and took the microphone from Suzy. He couldn't resist a pirouette, despite looking like he'd been dragged out of the Sticky Sundown Swamp.

'Ahem,' Clive said into the microphone. 'Right. Well, I suppose you think I'm up here to have a tantrum.'

The crowd nodded and murmured.

'Well, I'm not,' said Clive. 'Although I really want to, because I should have been chosen as the Special Guest and now my tutu is ruined . . .' He growled but then stopped himself. 'But having nice clothes isn't enough to make you

happy. What makes you happy is friendship. And there's a group of friends here today that have made me feel a bit different.'

Pip leaned over to Lucky. 'Whatever is the Glamour Gang up to now?' she whispered.

Clive continued. 'These friends said to me that I didn't have to impress and win in life. I just had to be kind and enjoy the gift of friendship.' He sniffed. 'Well, there's something my Aunt Augusta used to say – spread the surprise sunshine of smiles. And so today, on the sunniest day of the year, I want you to look at the cute next to you and give them your best smile. Your cutest smile. A smile that says, I'm glad you're my friend.'

Suzy looked shocked, but she nodded. 'Go on, everyone. Do as Clive says.'

The cutes began to pass smiles around like presents, one person to the next person, until the whole field was smiling. Lucky found that Clive was passing his smile to her.

'This is what I wanted to say earlier, before I was attacked by popcorn,' Clive said.

Lucky blushed. Clive was still giving her a big warm smile that showed his row of funny little teeth! And she smiled right back. Everyone was laughing and grinning. The hunger in their tummies was replaced with warm bubbles of friendship.

'And now for the Friendship Horn!' Suzy cheered.

Krissy the kite came on to the stage, dragging a large ice-cream cone. She lifted it with difficulty and blew with all her might. There was a trumpeting sound, followed by a flock of startled cornetti birds which had been

nesting in the cone all year.

The super cutes settled down on their picnic blankets. Lucky stayed where she was, staring at Clive.

'Are you okay, Lucky?' Cami whispered by her ear. 'You look a bit shocked.'

Lucky nodded. 'I just . . . I can't believe it,'

she said. 'I've been showing Clive kindness for so long, hoping that one day he would show some kindness back. Today, I was ready to give up. I thought it would never make a difference. But it's happened! I've done it, Cami! I've made that grumpy little chihuahua understand the joy of being friendly!'

'Well done, Lucky,' Pip said.

'You were right all along,' Cami said kindly. 'It just shows you should never give up.'

'If the day starts with friendship and ends with friendship, then that is a very good day indeed,' said Sammy.

Happiness welled up inside Lucky and made her heart flutter and her mane quiver.

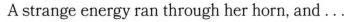

A strange energy ran through her horn, and . . .

GASP!

Everyone shrieked with amazement as fizzy rainbow ribbons streamed from Lucky's horn. They scattered far and wide, wrapping themselves around each slice and bowl of treats in neat little bows. A friendship gift for everyone at the festival!

The cutes munched the treats and chewed the fizzy bows and the air zipped and zapped with feel-good vibes.

'Oh, Lucky, you're marvellous!' Pip said, grabbing two ribbons and trying some dance gymnastics. She immediately lost her balance and fell into a family of bristle-back hodgepogs.

But no one knew who had prickled whom, so they all rolled around laughing.

With the air full of song and laughter, ribbons and bunting and banners, the Friendship Festival was feeling just as the Friendship Festival should. The cutes told jokes and stories. Then they took turns remembering how they first met. Sammy's fur turned sunshine yellow as he told the story of making friends with Pip, Cami and Lucky in a sunflower field. Dee produced some cake to re-enact meeting them all at the Blossom Festival, when she had her paws full of refreshment muffins. And Micky blushed as he remembered being a bit bossy when he first met them at the museum.

They laughed and chatted round their picnic
blanket. It was the longest day of summer, and
they were going to make the most of it.

Dee created fruit-shaped felt beanbags to
throw and catch. Sammy told them every fact
he knew about festivals in the World of Cute
– at least, until he fell asleep on Cami's soft
fluff! Louis sketched the highlights of the day in
a little book. Pip practised her pineapple rolls,
helped by Suzy, who was a master at rolling

sideways. Neither of them was as good at rolling as Micky and his team of brothers and sisters, though.

The sun started to dip and the sky turned the colour of apricot jam. Jelly flamingos flew overhead and the evening swarms of flitterlings and glow-bugs scattered rose-gold light across the field. The Festival was mellow and golden, and the friends sang songs of kindness and love in the lamplight of the nearby sunflowers, and everything was good.

'I've got a lovely snuggly warm feeling in my tummy,' Lucky said.

'Friendship is the best hot-water bottle,' Cami said.

'Hot, urgh!' Pip said. 'I hate the heat. How about we say friendship is cool, instead?'

Lucky laughed. 'All right then. Let's just say friendship is great, whatever the weather.'

'It's such a perfect evening, I don't want it to end,' said a little voice. Clive! The second-chance chihuahua shuffled into a space at the picnic blanket and blinked at everyone happily.

The sun disappeared and the moon rose. Its lunar glow made Lucky's horn light up, and the milky light spread all around them.

'I don't have to be home until it gets dark,' Sammy said. 'And strictly speaking, it's not dark now, is it?'

Louis nodded. 'That's a fact.'

The cutes laughed. And at last, as they sleepily made their way home, they sang their song.

Friendship Festival, what a day!
The Super Cute friends know
how to play!
One, two, three, hip hip hooray!

Clive joined in. And although his singing voice was not the best, no one minded. Because for some reason, on this occasion, it sounded really quite cute.

CAUSING CHAOS IN A WORLD OF CUTE!

SUPER CUTE

THE ADVENTURE SCHOOL

PIP BIRD

Here's an exclusive extract of the next exciting Super Cute book, out NOW!

CHAPTER ONE

All Aboard the Ramen Ride!

It was morning in the World of Cute and honey-coloured sunshine streamed through the bedroom window of Dee the dumpling kitty. She yawned and reached for her wakey-cakey – a delicious strawberry and cream-filled donut topped with popping candy. She took a large bite, and with a pop on her tongue and a tingle in her tum, she began to fill with energy.

Dee needed all the energy she could get. She had been up late, crafting, and her mind had refused to go to sleep as it was buzzing with the excitement of tomorrow.

Now tomorrow was today!

She stretched out her paws and then leaped out of bed. Pinned to the cork board above her crafting desk were the sashes and bows she'd made the night before. And stacked on the tabletop were little caps, each embroidered with the letters CC.

"Camp Cute!" Dee cried with happiness. "It's time to go to Camp Cute!" She rolled around on the floor with excitement and then jumped to her feet. "What am I thinking? There's no time to lose. I have to pack!"

Dee never went anywhere with empty pockets. You never knew when something might need making, or fixing, or decorating. And this weekend it was *extra* important. She and her friends, the super cutes, were on their way to Camp Cute Adventure School, where there would be activities and adventures and lessons about caring for the environment. They'd be staying the night, too. Emergency crafting supplies was essential.

Dee gathered balls of wool. She folded felt squares and rolled up materials and pushed

them deep into her pockets. She collected her brushes and pouches of paint. And what about clay? And glue and pins and sequins? Today of all days, she didn't want to run out of supplies. She pushed and packed everything as tightly as she could, but it was no good.

Although her fluffy pockets were deep and stretchy, they couldn't carry everything.

"Oh, I can't make it fit!" she wailed.

Make it . . . That was it!

"If you can't make something happen, then make something that'll help!" Dee exclaimed to herself.

She scoffed the rest of the wakey-cakey and licked the crumbs from her whiskers. Then she grabbed some quick-drying clay. Working quickly with her paws to pull, stretch and shape it, she created a lightweight box. Then she added canvas straps. Hmm. It wasn't quite good enough . . .

A second later, with the help of some paints, Dee had turned the box into a sturdy rainbow-coloured backpack!

"That's better!" Dee said. "Ready, set, go!"

Dee placed her crafting materials inside the bag and swung it over her back. Then she clipped the bows she'd made all over her fur.

"Accessorising is everything," she purred.

"CAMP CUTE, HERE I COME!"

Dee skipped all the way to the Wish Tree meeting place, where her super cute friends were already waiting. They clapped and whistled when they saw her coming.

"Hi everyone!" Dee said. "Sorry I'm late. I had to create!"

"You look amazing!" Lucky said, smiling.

"You do, too," Dee replied. "*All* of you!"

Dee noticed that Lucky the lunacorn was wearing the rainbow-striped leg-warmers she'd made her for her birthday, and a tutu too! In fact, everyone was bright and colourful. Cami the cloud, Louis the labradoodle, Micky the mini-pig, Pip the pineapple: they all wore anoraks, bags and wellies in bright fruit-salad colours of pink, red, orange and green. Even Sammy the sloth had orange glasses on, and a compass hung around his neck.

"Here, I made you all something," Dee

said, handing out the monogrammed caps and sashes.

"We look so C-C-CUTE!" Lucky laughed.

"Of C-C-COURSE we do!" Pip giggled.

"C-C-CAN we go now?" Micky said, pretend-seriously.

"Camp Cute here we come!" Cami said, raining down little inflatable maracas, which rattled before bursting with a pop and a squeal.

Check out more adventures with the Super Cutes!

CAUSING CHAOS IN A WORLD OF CUTE!

SUPER CUTE

BEST FRIENDS FOREVER

PIP BIRD

CAUSING CHAOS IN A WORLD OF CUTE!

SUPER CUTE

THE SLEEPOVER SURPRISE

YOU ARE INVITED

PIP BIRD

Enjoyed Super Cute? Check out these other brilliant books by Pip Bird!

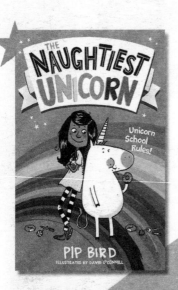

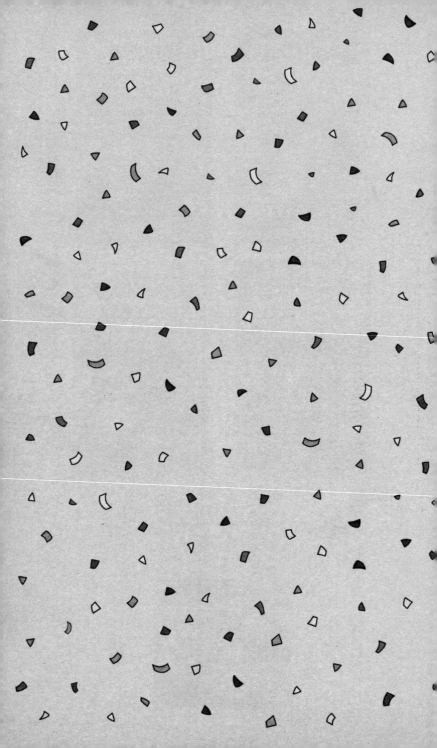